TEX
The Cowboy

A Red Fox Book

Published by Random House Children's Books
20 Vauxhall Bridge Road, London SW1V 2SA

A division of Random House UK Ltd
London Melbourne Sydney Auckland
Johannesburg and agencies throughout the world

Copyright © Sarah Garland 1995

1 3 5 7 9 10 8 6 4 2

First published in Great Britain by
The Bodley Head Children's Books 1995

Red Fox edition 1997

The right of Sarah Garland to be identified as the author and
illustrator of this work has been asserted by her in accordance
with the Copyright, Designs and Patents Act, 1988

Printed in Singapore
by Tien Wah Press (Pte) Ltd

RANDOM HOUSE UK Limited Reg. No. 954009

ISBN 0 09 926701 2

TEX
The Cowboy

Sarah Garland

Red Fox

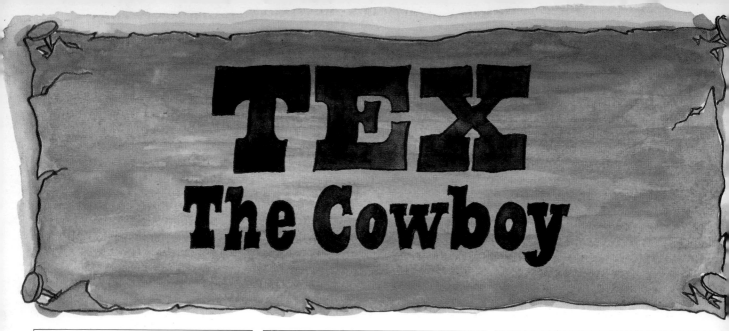

TEX
The Cowboy

Tex the cowboy is asleep.

The sun comes up.

Tex puts on his trousers

and his shirt and waistcoat

and his boots

and his scarf

TEX
and Gloria

Tex the cowboy goes singing down the trail.

Home, home on the range...

We need some money, Gloria

Tex and Gloria think about food.

They see a notice on a cactus.

TEX
and the Hold-Up

This is the stage coach bound for Laramie.

But there is a problem.

No one will ride shotgun.

But who is this riding into town?   It is Cowboy Tex and his horse, Gloria.

TEX
and the Gold Rush

Tex and Gloria are trying to sleep.

But there is too much noise!

It is morning.

Tex and Gloria look up 'Gold Digging'.

First they try panning.

Then they try sieving.

Then they try hammering.